T0067997

I CAN'T

FOR LOSING

JOHN TARPLEY

author**HOUSE**®

AuthorHouse™
1663 Liberty Drive
Bloomington, IN 47403
www.authorhouse.com
Phone: 833-262-8899

Published by AuthorHouse 07/28/2021

ISBN: 978-1-6655-3331-7 (sc)
ISBN: 978-1-6655-3330-0 (e)

Library of Congress Control Number: 2021915309

Print information available on the last page.

Chapter 1

One morning Marvin, woke up off to work and stop at cisco carwash when he walked in the parking lot Marvin, saw this beautiful woman pulled up in her Nissan Sentra and she got out of her vehicle he walked up to her to sell her some purses, movies, and cd's. Marvin asked her, what is your name? and she said Melody, as the author write about himself, and I told her my name was Marvin, he continues to sell products to her saying would you like to buy some of my things that I am selling. I was talking to Melody, in a happy way she said do you talk to all of your clients this way (laughing) (v1 Janet Jackson; doesn't really matter) and I said no; depending on who it is if it's a lady I respect them as a lady, if it's a gay man or women I respect them in a special way cause they more attention even for church people and for bitches and ho's, however, they come I respect them I don't discriminate they get served how they come. When he looked into Melody, eyes he questioned her about her man Melody responded that she was not ready for a man nor a relationship and I said a beautiful black Nubian princess like you should not be by yourself she looked at me and started smiling "you got good game" I told her game should not be ran on a grown woman that's a lady, he said the way you dress, the way your hair looks, your smile, your clean to me, the way you carry yourself, the way you talk and dress mostly all women don't come outside this way. Then Marvin, was curious for Melody number and she gave it to him for this reason, I started singing songs to her because she liked the cd's I was selling it was old school (v2 Surface; only you could make me happy) slow songs I am old school and Melody was too. For this reason, I was making her laugh more no one else made her laugh or smile I made her feel good while getting lost in the conversation Melody told me she has two kids. Her son's name is Thomas, and her daughter name is Teresa, Melody said I am not looking for no relationship I just would like to be friends because I am a teacher that goes to Barry University College I have been independent women staying strong for my kids and have big dreams also high standards reaching goals she said I will not let no one stop that.

I was surprise I looked at her and thought in my mind having chills speaking out of contents "girl you know you're a strong black woman."

After I have spoken she sat down where other customers was sitting down to get their car wash, most of them were women that was sitting at the car wash and two of them were men they were also sitting down next to these women. The other women were watching me sell to Melody they began to give me their number asking me for cd's slow songs the same ones Melody bought from me these women also purchased (v3 Beyonce ft. Chris brown; Jealous) purses all of my customers say that the products I have are good and they look real you're a good salesman, afterwards, Melody, said that I'm jealous your busy getting their number he said that's what I do I'm a salesman and then Marvin, says you shouldn't be worried about this because you just want to be friends right?

Then Melody looked at me begin laughing, so as I made sales my back turned from her she taps me on the shoulder give me your cell phone number (while giving her cell phone number) Marvin, told her call me later and continued walking around the corner going up a couple of blocks I left the car wash because my godmother lived a couple of blocks down the street from the car wash I told Melody bye. Melody, pulled out her cell phone to call "Marvin hey what are you doing later?" He says nothing when I get to my godmother I'll be chilling' in my room come see me at five o'clock I'll pay for dinner she replied my two kids are going to be with me so yeah later we check each other out [while driving her Benz] they talked for 40minutes about everything including love, sex, marriage, and then Marcus, mentioned a new video coming out pretty soon so if you want I can get that for you. She said where you at. He says I'm down the street from the car wash for someone that just left the car wash you called me fast it was quick well you're the only friend I know she said I'm outside boy where your crazy self at, he became vulnerable to her giving the location of his street Melody finally found the location she said hey playa I'm outside with my two kids she pulled up right on the side of me and open her car door: she said get in Marvin, disapprove right away you do not even know me there's crazy people in this world; I can be a killer or a rapist, stalker, or a perfect stranger she looked surprise and started to laugh. Marvin was very curious he asked her are you afraid of picking me up around the corner, she says no I'm not afraid I know your good for making me happy and laugh it's been a while since I've been happy so besides your mother do you have anybody else in your life, Marvin begin to joke letting Melody know that he put it down like that he still talking and then he says listen [as he put head phones in her ears] [v4 case; happily ever after] you wouldn't be in my car if I wasn't telling the truth so, while we was driving I ask Monica to take me to Walmart because I needed some movies and cd's from the store and she took me as we walked into the store I was telling her about who I was in business with two of my friends and also my business partners Cornelius and Juan. My aspiration for Melody has grown I felt comfortable letting her know where my business is on 79th street NW 27th Avenue across from Burger King and then the conversation led away about where her kids go to school at I told her a secret and it was that I could not have children because the medication that I have been taking for years had me messed up in my sperm cells. I told her I would like to have a son or a daughter, however, it was time to leave Walmart I loved Melody so much because she listens to my stories about how my mother was killed and how I have changed my live around afterwards, Melody dropped me home and then she went home but before she left we gave each other a hug and a kiss I said friends are not supposed to hug like that and then she pushed me away laughing saying [boy you so crazy] she pulled off and said good night see you tomorrow. The next day Melody took a break off her job just to come see me around the corner of 27th Avenue and 79st I had purses on me selling cd's and DVD's all day Melody pulled up in her car smiling hey baby I took the day off just to see you, are you hungry maybe around 3:00pm we get some-thing to eat I said m-a-a-n I didn't know friends come up on people like that so I seen her laughing she parked her car to speak with me I told my friend I have a surprise for her and she said what is it? I said turn your car radio on and put this cd in she said ok I said press number 7 on this disc and when the song came on I start singing the song to her it was a song by surface [v5 surface; can you stand the rain], as she listens he says what other ones you want to hear putting CDs' in a five-cd changer

[v6 Ciara; dance like were making love], [v7 Akon ft. sizzle, shabba ranks, vybz cartel; sole survivor], [v8 drug hill; 5 steps] it was songs by surface, Akon, dru hill, she said this is my song [bouncing her head back and forth] I like this song. Marvin a black brother who loved Nubian brown skin he showed her how to have fun, however, she had to leave Melody says you know my lunch break is over would you like to call you later he says yeah make sure you call me if you do not hit me up on my cell phone I will call you or drop by your crib she pulled off in her car. After work that day me, myself, and I went home to work on my project the phone rang it was Melody telling how much love and fear she got for me after that night I went to sleep.

My friend Cornelius and Juan met Melody after I got thru talking to my girl I ask Cornelius father to take me to see her, my friend Mr. Brown said to me I heard you got a woman as he jokes about its Marvin being a thug life ghetto fabulous brother that he is told Mr. Brown that she is just a friend. But one thing I did feel good about being a real man I stood up for myself and Melody when my friend Cornelius and Juan said to me man we bet you $500 dollars a piece that you have sex with that woman, your going have to tell her you love her, I'm not going bet with you all because she's a lady and they said alright ok we stop digging you m-a-a-n we leave you alone with Melody! But If you do get that sexy ass woman right there we will give you the money ha ha ha. I pulled up to Melody with Mr. Brown in his truck as I look at Mr. Brown speak fluently about how nice Melody is and how good she looks she fine as hell a Nubian Brazilian black queen Marvin, knowingly his thug life came with the tone of voice she is every color of every rose there it is! Melody was standing her beautiful ass daisy duets shorts with hills, and a nice pink blouse speaking foreign hey brother you came with your crew today what change your mind to come here with your crew I gave her a kiss baby one day you will be my women I am taking my time and patience, being nice taking the time to know you better. I am a man and I have become so wise about Melody that Mr. Brown got out the truck walked up to Monica and said to me where did you meet this beautiful woman and I said at the car wash, I told Mr. Brown I do not have to make any promises to her cause her smile and beauty is a smile all by itself; when I look at Melody to ask about her agenda for tomorrow she

Chapter 2

said nothing do you have any plans, I said how would you feel about dinner tomorrow I'll take us out at night Melody replied sure it's ok; the conversation continued to steam about love, life, kids, and we joke of adult things Melody mentioned to me that her daughter is 14 years old and her son is 10 years old their names are Thomas, and Teresa we looked at each other smiling and laughing then Melody said you brought this man with you to see me are you crazy, Mr. Brown said he had to go because he has to work in the morning therefore, I went home and gave Melody a kiss on the cheek; and I pause to tell her I would see her tomorrow and she said ok then I left; and in the morning I arose to go to work on 79th street on 27th Avenue the things I go through with people in the streets women, pimps, hoe's, bitches, sluts, homo sexual, gays, transvestites, hustlers, hookers, good, bad, angry, evil men, Christians all kinds of people happy or sad every day robbers stealers and killers; because I was out there in the streets thugging but I change for God, myself, a difference in change is for what best for living heart with love. But, when I was on the corner that day selling ladies purses, movies, cd's, perfumes, men cologne, watches and custom jewelry for ladies, men shoe almost everything. I was not out there stealing or selling drugs I am out here independent black afro American trying to make a living; standing on my feet with booths all day working for my father up above praying send love, money, power, holy art thou o lord do not let get killed underneath the sun working on the corner bless me always with a big house, and a car, with my lady in it. Then I called Monica on her cell phone curious if she is ready to go to dinner I took Melody to a nice restaurant it was called Benihana's, a Jamaican Bistro very pricey and upscale [V9 Janet Jackson; anytime, anyplace]. When I picked her up she looked beautiful in a nice Champaign dress with gold sequence that glow in the dark, when we walked in the restaurant sitting down chatting about us and what she does for a living Melody told me that she is a school teacher at Corbett Smith View Elementary her son Thomas goes to the same school and her daughter goes to Dear

Field Middle School amaze to see she's sitting in front of me dazing at her beauty he says I never kept a woman this long or dated anyone by my job. Managing a business is incredibly stressful. I sell mostly to women that invest to support me because when I was in business with men they set me up, tried to bring me down or ran off with my things. However, Melody wanted to know of my last broke up with my ex-wife Nancy, because she would call my phone and text my phone, play music and leave messages on my phone that was lies my ex-wife Nancy divorce me. I change my number hundreds of times, but it did not do good explaining my history to Melody, about making plans to save money to open a bigger business, Melody said at least you are not out there robbing and stealing. She looked at me and said I would not do you like that I can handle it if I do not see you cheating on me, I told Melody, that is what they all say, then when I get into the relationship it be a different story. They kiss while getting separate plates to eat and separate drinks the conversation continued to rise telling my girlfriend about my house in Miami Gardens it is a two-bedroom house Melody, told me she lives with her mother and her furniture was in storage. We ordered our food and it was cook right in front of us me and Melody was smiling, laughing together; pressing my lips on hers telling her of my mother Cynthia Brooks who passed away I told her that my father was sick with cancer my name is Luis Robles, we ate our food it was good and then after we finish eating she try to seduce me telling me to go back to school and get a G. E. D. to start a new career come out of the streets. My thoughts of Melody, were right I press my lips against hers started kissing my hands upon her thighs she is gorgeous my pretty lady ask what do you like? I told her modeling, acting, singing, and church we were full Melody, ask did you have a good time in the car I said yeah I was just about to ask you the same thing. I thought friends was not supposed to call each other baby she said you can let it go I am not afraid to say baby to someone I think is incredibly special he started to exaggerate on the comment that she made they cannot help themselves there carefully in love other people cannot see it but them in the shadow they please each other with words like baby, sugar, and cream. As they laugh together and joke she started having fun with him they push each other around then the words came out I have never met a man that makes me laugh as much as you did. I looked at her and said we'll I love you as a friend do you want to take it to the next level or still be friends, Melody, still a thug using slang to talk to Melody saying I told you I love you I didn't say I was in love with you because that would be a lie how I'm going to be in love with someone who I'm just getting to know he said didn't god say love everyone and Melody said your right that is true. I drove her home that day and before she got out the car we exchange kiss to me it was like a friendly kiss desperate for her lips I grab her and kiss her stroke my hands through her Brazilian hair she is a beautiful woman. Melody said my birthday is coming up pretty soon which is in two weeks, I said when is it she said July 25, 1973 and I said well I have to surprise a friend and Melody said you stop saying that if you're ready to be my lady Melody continue yapping about her birthday relating to being a real strong black woman I respect myself I told her listen don't have me waiting let's just do this and we be good alright I want you to have a wonderful birthday your worth the wait looking at your sexy body long layered hair pinned up, and Kiyonna lace dress; beige underneath with beige pumps; smoky eye shadow; pink plum lip gloss; red cheek color; Brazilian mocha skin color, Melody, reply I got to go my feet are killing I'm tired and I have to take a bath and then I'm going to sleep Marvin, being tired with her said be ready for work tomorrow good night and he went home, incidentally I reach home I was thinking to myself now is this the woman that will accept what I do, and accept who I am is she going to runaway and get angry or frustrated? So, I call my boy Juan on his cell phone just to tell him there might be a lady for me and I think she's the one I want to be with his cell phone ring he said "hello" hey what up this Marvin what you doing you got time for me Juan replied No, why is there something wrong Marvin said look I want to talk to you about Melody I think that she's the one for me and I tried to make her happy her birthday is coming up and I just don't know what to do. Juan said get her some-thing nice and take her out dinner make her feel good, Melody felt alone for the night just talking of how his body hurt and back is starting to be painful I need muscle relaxer I was trying to get into massage spa down at south beach then I could take her to the movies after wards, Juan feeling resentment said that is a Great idea yeah sure anything to get you out of bed alright

I got to go just take it slow do not move to fast. Then I decided to take a long bath thinking of her she was better than Nancy praying of my father that he brings me a good woman that would like my work and ethnicity someone I can cherish and hold forever. However, I said the lord's prayer first and said amen went to sleep. The next morning my work had to produce it was time for me to stand in the hot sun selling cd's, movies, perfumes making a way for all my children, women and I still must help my ex-wife thinking of her made me feel good she liked what I like whenever we argue it stopped then we kiss.

My boys were out there with me selling on the corner Charles, Timothy, Joseph and Samuel. Charles sold purses, shoes he was in the hustling game before I even came out he was a brother who motivated me to get out there other than my father, mother and uncle. I was hustling since I was 12 years old, Timothy worked for Charles, Joshua sold pictures on the gate. Samuel sold socks, clothes, lighters, and other things like hats I liked Jonathan slogan his topic was loud he will say out loud to the customers passing by do not let your socks get down to the nitty gritty looking all black; stank; and shitty holla at your boy at sock city! But mine slogan was if you do not get your purses; perfume; cologne; movies; cd's; somebody else will, we got them for our happy and angry customers. I also had ladies working for me as a business partner her name is Margret she is incredibly beautiful afro American, tall, long legs sexy legs, weave in her head extensions, make up is to die for, close-set eyes that glows and nice lips when she talks her voice sounds like Janet Jackson. She would sell purses for me to anybody at her job or her friends from home now I also have another woman working for me her name is Ms. Rose she also sales purses and perfumes on her job or at church remembering the good work she done for me Ms. Rose had pass away of breast cancer she works at McDonalds I also had my cousin Terry working for me on the same corner on 79th street and 27th Avenue. I would do this every day because this is what I do for a living it made me feel good I was not out there killing, robbing, stealing, or selling drugs I sold coach bags, Louis Vuitton, Prada, Dohoney and Burke, Channel, Gucci, (v10 august Alina ft. Nicki Minaj; no love) listening to music at the same time selling all kinds of purses whether it be Dereon, Fendi, Dolce Gabbana etc. Well, any I had a lot of customers plenty people was jealous of me and still are until this day because I was coming up making better plans for myself. My friend Charles wife sold with us too, in my mind I'm still thinking of Melody, wondering when can I hit that (v11 august Alina; testify) I called Melody everyday when I was at work and at home I can't give in she's the one for me my heart is falling for her man she has a booty like Lil Kim you, I took brakes from work just thinking of her beauty she's ready like a porn star I was so busy moving around trying to sell and making this money for me and my lady and what hurt me the most is not giving the lord our savior Jesus Christ his ten percent of earnings of what I made on the corner so that I can keep getting blessed periodically, I called Melody on her cell phone as I'm walking on the corner selling products from Jay Enterprises while on the phone with her she said "I'm going out there to meet with you do you need anything to eat" I said looking at the way I work, me and you will take a bubble bath when we get home. I got in her car we drove to a hotel since I had a lot of loot we took our time and had lunch at the lobbyist hotel in a five star Doubletree Hotel it was a wonderful night Melody, says do you want to know how the cookie taste my response was girl let's go upstairs now I'm hard she was very pretty in her tight pants, black hills, embroidered shirt with bling on it as soon as we went in our hotel room she took off her clothes I'm sitting down jaw dropping looking at her climb on top of me it's too good to be true it felt like a Porn Movie, Melody and Marvin have sex in August Alina words this is a Benediction (v12 fantasia Barrino; bittersweet) I thought the night was over I took it to the next level telling Melody I got something to show you she said what (he pulled out his diploma) I decided to take your advice so what's the next step Melody began to sing a song from the album "Sam Smith" called stay with me and she said sell your business instead sing or rap he said all women like the way I run my business but there would be times on the streets men will cut me fight me for my business because it's booming and hell would catch me feeling the pressure from Juan, Cornelius, and sometimes Terry the list goes on and on Timothy, Charles I take them to be like family they going be thugs for life ingas be crazy shit fucking ho's and bitches after close shop. Joshua is a nonbeliever, but he helps through pain their days

I got shot and bleed almost to death they call the police for me trust and believe I was saved I almost forgot my homeboy Daniel who is an employer for Jay Enterprises some days he would come out there and work for me. Charles, Timothy, made the streets every color, race, and origin people would come buy from us whether it be blacks, Haitians, Cubans, Whites, but in the hustling game I never seen color as a problem I saw a human race that I never discriminated I loved everyone well Melody brought her kids to come see me her beautiful daughter Teresa and her handsome son Thomas I close my business down the next day just to go to the movies with them this is what it means to be with family how to grow in the spirit teaching love to our children is very important author, the meaning of family meant a lot to Marvin knowing how his family came apart and he never had kids that were so smart and uplifting compare to his ex-wife always complaining, murmur, the type that loves to instigate problems bringing back thugs from the streets to her house hoeing in the house in front of the kids sometimes the author will say get a grip teach your kids how to have education but Nancy didn't care she see it like I'm the only one taking care of my kids so why not let sell myself short let me be a bitch fucking ingas for their money and drugs. Marvin had a good time bringing them to the movies but at the same time he is worried about his kids with Nancy he that she is good for prostituting in front of them she has not been around the knows corner selling purses, perfumes, and movies wondering in his mind where the hell she at? Anyway, we had a good time neither one of their fathers cared for them Thomas feeling hopeless without a father he was nowhere to be found Tyler never saw his father but today they shall not struggle through pain they got me as their father. When Teresa father got Melody pregnant he was not with her and he did not care for her, so I am here to give myself a pat on the back it is what a real man do, on our way going home I played music for her to let Melody know she is my girl I will never change (v13 Ciara ft. 50 cents; cannot leave alone) my ambition is to always make my girl happy there's no change of heart my character is to be a father and a husband and it's all about keeping my dick in my pants Melody is not ready for marriage just yet after she drop me home me and hr shared a kiss I'm still feeling the need to splurge trying to hold it down I fell for her my girl Kimberly Michelle was right a well known author of Pain Medicine titled "feels like I'm falling" telling Melody I love you too much it kills me to be far apart from you please one day give more than a kiss I really want to try to have kids lets work on seeing a doctor alright baby being surprise Melody is speechless ok baby I'll make an appointment with the doctor try to keep yourself out of trouble. Author, Melody was hurt before from his boys and his ex now that he found the true one he's holding it down people can ask a question how many times will a man cheat or will he keep lying (grinning) come to see me tomorrow I (tears) I-I- I'm speechless you think I'm the one for you sweetie lets work on it ok just because we live apart doesn't mean you can't call me soon my plans to move in with you as your husband yeah give me a hug (V14 Kimberly Michelle; how many times) a lady time is not to be wasted she could be doing other things with her time Marvin wasn't confuse as to whom he'll see saying come anytime bring Thomas so we can play video games and I can teach him how to be a man., called Marvin on his cell phone because he was curious about Jane wondering where she's at his cell phone rings Marvin "hello" wink said hey nigga do you know where Jane is? I tried calling her cell phone but there's no answer could you call her for me it's time for me to close the shop and she suppose to come here and bring the money in so that I can give her more purses and perfumes to sell, he said listen Jane is at work her customers will see her at the show her job is doing a promotion she'll bring you the money tomorrow, wink is not convince he says you sure she's not with you nigga fuck why didn't nobody say anything to me shit fucking tired he said no she's not with me I haven't seen her all day alright nigga wink you there he replies yeah (looking shock while on the phone; wink) where could she have gone let me know if she call you (music playing in the background at his home (v15 Kimberly Michelle ft. R. Kelly; you and I) he hangs up his cell phone. Now Jane enters his home quite late and says the kids kept me up baby I am sorry wink do you want something sugar he says your late I called Marvin asking him about you where you were at baby you know the time for me to spend with my lady is you. She said my job is doing a new promotion deal I had to be there here's the money yeah wink looking tugged out in his baggy pants, t-shirt, timberland boots, wavy short hair, mocha skin tone color feeling good now that he saw Jane they kiss get ready for me tonight so we can work on us go head the room in their I'll be back I have to close the shop Charles couldn't close the shop because he went to court so did rock they got in trouble for something they did. Back to Marvin a thug out nigga that has been living in hood for a long time being hurt but now that he's met a woman it will be the first lesson learn for all the men out there take notes it's not a pain killer he told Melody bring Teresa you've been hanging out with me we could have a family picnic she said no because I still don't know you that well I don't want her father to come at me for bringing me

Chapter 3

daughter to another man's house, it is my conscious I am afraid of who I introduce my daughter to I just do not trust no one around my daughter or my son ok bye baby we will be there tomorrow Marvin damn I wish I could fuck her (as he speaks to himself walking away from Melody). Melody pulls away from his driveway and she call her cousin Kimberly just to explain to her about their relationship, but one thing Kimberly was always jealous of her the problem with Kimberly is she did not have money to take care of her family her man was a loser working in the streets her sales drugs to make ends meet sometimes the money just comes up short her cell phone rings Kimberly answers "hello" who is this? Melody said it is me girl (tone: happy) let me tell you my man is fly wow I cannot explain a million hearts hell over I gave it my heart Kimberly on the phone sounding frustrated and envy please tell me you are not calling to say that you are listening to Kimberly Michelle Pate- a million hearts. Monica said no, w-h-a-t the girl me and my man will be moving in together and were planning on getting marriage counsel we've been dating and I want to take it to the next level so what do you think if I need a girl to walk down the aisle will you be my girl Kimberly replies hell no that nigga is not a good man just leave it alone ok I don't think he's going be faithful to you and he doesn't enough back ground to get a loan to open a shop fuck that bullshit nigga you need a man that will buy you a house and a boat come back to me when you're sure about finding a new man. Marvin, called Melody after he finished talking to Juan about his woman he tells her you're a strong black woman a blessing to have an angel, Melody said how sweet well I'll be sleeping now so we talk later boo, I walked back into my house took a bath watch television until I fell asleep Marvin, had got up the next morning he did not go to work he got up brush his teeth put on some clothes Melody, called him like 10 times his cell phone was on silent he called her back and she said I thought you forgot about me and he said no I didn't forget who my people are and she said I'm on my way over there and I said ok. She came over my house and brought her son Thomas Melody also bought food with her so that we can have lunch leaving her daughter with her mother anyway we watched sports and movies at the house and Tyler remind me that Melody's birthday is coming up soon. I turn my back to Melody and said I have a surprise she said what is it? It wouldn't be a surprise if I told you Melody, lol then we left to get something to eat, we went to Red Lobster we ate some good food I looked at Melody, and her son Thomas he took pictures from my cell phone we all was smiling, love, I ask Thomas what college did you want to go to and he said I don't know yet, and I ask him what did you want to be when you grow up, Thomas answered a "pilot". Thomas is very educated I don't want nothing getting in the way of his future or his career I learn from the best my father could not teach me so now I'm teaching how to be a man he'll never have to suffer after we left Red Lobster we both went to the park I was telling Melody, while Thomas play that braking up with my ex- wife was a very terrible thing love have never felt so good putting trust first but because of the business I run she could never trust me it's hard to keep a woman. The business that I run can be dangerous because you must be on the street corner Melody reply she could trust me wait until we move in do you think your ex-wife would mine because I am in love with a good man he has got everything I need I wrap my arms around a strong man missing you would be hard to do baby, Marvin, grab and kiss her the surprise is under the sheets at home baby lets go home so you can unravel your present I am a Kazillionaire sweetie it is not hard I am just a phone call away she answered to me when I put this pretty little thing on you what you going to do. He says sugar, honey, I do it for you let me put it on you. *(Kimberly Michelle Pate- Hard to do)* Marvin, said I would not think your sleeping with someone else baby situations are different for me ok I could not treat like that if your honest with me honey, as Thomas was playing on the playground I gave her one look do not worry and then we left home so she can unravel her present on our way home Melody, was talking to me about Barry University the college she goes to. It was getting late ok Melody must go to school tomorrow I said alright Melody dropped me home and said I will be back to unravel my present let me drop off Thomas to my mother's they both said bye; and we love you I said I love you too. Therefore, I went in my house and I took a bath when I got out of the shower I prayed, and I turned on the radio *(Fantasia Barrino- 2 weeks' notice)* my future could never go dead if I got god in my life (Monica came back for her special present) we stayed in bed until the next morning I woke up and went to work remembering to get breakfast at Burger King. Wow, I suffered through pain, betrayal, I learned not to give Satan glory! That day was a beautiful day weeks went by and I was thinking we're all guilty of pleasure no one is perfect ok it was still Melody's birthday I took her out to eat I looked at her the words just came out of my mouth I can't win for losing, if I lied to you then this relationship is not honest I pulled out my money $1,000 and gave it to her so she could spend some time with me and shop for herself and the kids I bought her some flowers and I gave her more money $500.00 we had good time Monica told me I love you they kiss none of her baby fathers ever did this I'm the first *(Kelly Price-you should've told me)* Melody decided to take me to a hotel after dinner and we made love to each other she surprised me, we made love all night Kimberly called my cell phone she sound depress I told her not to worry cause I'll explain it to Melody, then maybe we'll drop by she said come alone. I took her clothes off slowly rubbing her stomach slowly and softly I rubbed her breast and her nipples I was holding her like a dove I laid her down and rubbed her back also licked it she licked on my neck we kissed and fucked all night we went to sleep holding each other we woke up that next morning we made love again and again one thing I knew that this strong black woman did not want a two minute brother she wanted to be held and satisfied if I didn't come correct with a full package with everything I couldn't come at all; I'm not talking about making love or having sex it's about making a real woman wait respecting her, treating her right, not beating on her, taking care of her understanding her, honesty, loyalty, the responsibility and I did all of that I never thought I would be with Melody and she never thought she would never meet me. One thing I did know is that we sinned because we made love and we was not married god did not like that, after we made love that morning we took a bubble bath, I told her happy birthday over and over even thou it was a new day everyday is a new day a birthday for Melody. Having fun with her is like diamonds being looked at and shinning after we got through looking at each other and talking we got out the tub I help Melody put on her clothes I had some more surprise I gave her an expensive jewelry a necklace worth $850.00 I put it around her neck it goes with those jeans, clogs platform, and a blouse going across her cold shoulder she went to get her hair done that day I put my clothes waiting for her to get her nails done I pay for everything with the money I gave for her birthday she comes first and always will be my pride and joy then I took her to IHOP for breakfast, lunch Melody said your too much you need to stop I was so happy giving her my regression I said why? You do not always get this treatment that is why, I hook you up I had fun with her it was millions of roses every falling from the skies she was the center piece of my blessings

(v16 Fantasia Barrino-lose to win) also at Melody's house anywhere she may be I guaranteed she will see a thousand roses guess what right into my wedding I put her picture on my dresser we ate leaving IHOP, lol, we went to my house and made love again, no one look at me for who I was and it took me a while to look down the right road I am not ashamed of who I am and who I become. During our time together David called my cell phone wanting to know about Melody I told him please do not act stupid we just came from making love now we on the couch. Author, well Marvin listen to her heart it never felts so good, her heart beats just like his they laid on the couch and talk about marriage counselor after that they fell asleep they woke up two hours later feeling empty because their relationship is moving slow he feels strongly about her but she wanted more than just words Melody, wanted to have a wedding to invite people that love her and supported her to be there he's feeling happy because his book coming out and business is booming listening to Melody has kept him from trouble. Marvin looked at Melody and said baby you can go home and check on the kids, he told her good night gave her a kiss they both separated a couple of weeks later he went by her house to see the kids and check on Melody for the first time her mother saw me, but she does not like Marvin in his own words (slang language) where is my boo I need my baby is she here? Melody sounding happy hey king what's up it's been a while why didn't you call me sweetie her mother said well when you two decide to make adjustments to move in let me know, Melody didn't tell her mother yet but that day she talked to her mother "mamma um yeah he's here to help me pack" were moving out a month from now Tracy wasn't expecting to hear that so soon but she is happy for them both yeah people learn from their mistakes she says to her daughter and gave her a hug sugar I'm going to miss you please be careful because he lives a dangerous life I pray that he leaves his ghetto thug attitude at the streets don't bring that home to my daughter she deserves more than that. Melody, mamma thank you for approving and were having a wedding Marvin has not propose yet but he will soon ok Tracy could not believe it come to the back we're having a family party months later Melody moved in with me in my house my friends who I was in business with Juan and Cornelius helped me move her things out of storage Melody was indecisive of her daughter moving in with us because Melody wasn't ready for her daughter to move in with another man yet I told her god is love respect is due to those that pray. Her son Thomas and I helped her unpacked clothes, boxes, that we brought in from the storage (v17 Beyonce Knowles- if I were a boy) and then we kissed finally I couldn't believe I got the chance to share my possibility to Melody my beloved we've finished unpacking everything that was for Melody and kids clothes, shoes, belts, socks and her son Thomas things, well I felt good because I found a woman who could trust me of the work I do because every woman I had in the past couldn't be with me Melody's mother Tracy did not like me because in the past I went to prison back in 1996 she did not want her daughter with me Melody's mother was a Sergeant for south Florida Prison but now she's retired she said I got tired of seeing inmates being treated unfairly and killing each other for toilet or smokes she couldn't live with the guilt then she cried I went tissue to see her just to hear what she had to say about Melody Tracy ask me did you find a ring for my beautiful daughter are you planning to get an event planner for the wedding in the future I have made some calls with some of my peoples that will do everything for less price they won't charge for hidden fees, and surcharge. I replied no, the time has come for me to have marriage counselor we have been going strong for two years now I believe Melody will choose the event planner and all the expenses is on her cause I gave her the money, I gave Tracy her respect I hug her letting this woman know I change my life around your daughter will be safe with me. Author, even though Tracy had a attitude Marvin still showed her respect because she is human and beautiful woman like Melody's mom deserves better until this day a man must keep his mind right so he can walk down aisle or should I say sow what you reap during the time of harvest, a woman must deliver her labor like delivering a baby from its womb as the author I admire what Marvin which is also known as Jay, is trying to do he is keeping the peace between his fiancé and her mother. Marvin met Melody's grandmother her name is Gloria she is a sweetheart she love him and accept him like he was her own child she talk to him for hours and hours the most thing she talk about was Jesus Christ and I'm a part of this family always is and forever more Monica's mother doesn't see it that way Marvin being the thug that he is will continue exaggerating the fact he is marrying Melody in his life he says I met Melody's auntie Jennifer she did not like me neither but I love them all because that's all I wanted to have in my life that I never got before it's my family. Well me and Melody lived together and it was beautiful she's my angel we went to church together a lot but now I realize my fiancé moved in without getting married we stop getting marriage counseling because of all the movement it was last minute it hit me in my heart "money" something I don't have right now plus the guest list goes on forever we stayed as lovers boyfriend and girlfriend, well the whole time staying together at first it was sweet then we had our ups and downs, good days and bad days, we still stuck by each other's side. Look at me I am a man that do not have no family, so if bad times go bad the person I had was Melody. I love Melody because she is sweet and soft, humble, gentle, kind, likely, smart, nice and a strong back bone woman. Well, me and Melody son went to the movies and the youth fair we did fun things together she even came on the corner with me to sale purses, perfumes, one day I surprise

Chapter 4

Melody on her job I ordered a fruit basket to be placed on her desk I put a card in her car she does not know it is there when she came off from work her eyes pop open wide as she went to the car finding that card to her.

I had gave her a big fruit basket well when her and Thomas came home she jumped on top of me and hug and kissed me and licked me I fell on the ground there's no control of the emotions I was happy while she's on top of me I felt good the love made me have happy tears Melody's slow love is the only thing that touch me and made me talented, gifted, smart, intelligent, strong, now feeling deeply in love I told her listen to this (while he puts on blue tooth); (Brandy ft. Beyonce "Slow Love") as she shakes her head back and forth this song was in my heart for a year when it came out I was on the street corner selling them like crazy it made number one on the billboards. I got up off the floor slow dancing with Melody in my living room choosing to be good with her so tonight I can hit that and get some cream I received a call from Jane she wanted to know if I was coming back to work to give the inventory slip to her because someone at her job wanted to buy perfumes, purses, and movies I said Jane please ok the slips are in the car or inside the shop if you don't see them ask wink or rock, then she said Kimberly was looking for you and the slips are not there alright; so I had to cut my time short with Melody because just to send her the slips I believe they are in the car but I am the only one with the keys. Then I remembered to call dirty red and ask him to give Jane the slips (as he pulls out his cell phone) he calls Samuel "hello" [music in background] (Brandy Norwood-teller) Jay says what you doing' you see Jane over there he said no, what you need I have things to do yeah, can you give Jane the inventory slips for the purses, perfumes, and movies because someone in her job wants to purchase from us. He said she didn't come here so I'll talk to wink about it ok [he hangs up] Melody looked at me crying and smiling at the same time baby that was nice of you I got in the car and found the card sweetie Thomas couldn't believe how big it is he said mom if it's real can I have some of it [on the next track music is still playing Brandy- doesn't really matter] then Melody said to Thomas sure baby looking back at it jumping and bouncing in the living room saying yes, Thomas ask me where it came from? And I said your father. While we in bed I told her what all the fruits in the basket meant, I said baby all these things are fruits and gifts from god let him give it to you the fruits of thy labor, you are the fruits of my life the apples are the heart that you have for god, the apples cover the beautiful titties you have; the heart of thine eye lives longer than life itself. I looked at her and said the grapes are for the big pretty brown eyes the grapes you eat is the juice that comes out of them it is just like the tears coming down your face when I tell you I love you holding your face close to mines feeling the tears running down my hands let me kiss you press on your luscious lips, licking your neck tasting the same grape juice on your lips then I said Melody baby the banana is for when I watch you eat it and the way you open your mouth for that banana just like when I slide your dick in your mouth when we make love you click on my dick. Remembering how you eat the banana yeah, m-m-m, it taste good especially when you make love to me sucking on my dick like you do that banana thrusting it, in and out, your words yeah baby do you like it when I stroke the banana is it good sugar please hurt me with this banana exposing our love to the world letting them know how the sun shine even all around come right in I'm not going nowhere. The pineapples are the juice in your pussy and comes running out the cum taste like pineapples wet, silky, the pineapples are place on your plate [songs still playing Brandy-when u touch me]

For you to eat baby whenever I take you out to eat in a fancy restaurant Melody love her some daiquiri with alcohol and she pick the pineapple cut in cubes one by one as Melody eat it slow takes off the plate holding the glass in her hand asking me do you want a piece baby putting it in my mouth (slow motion) I gave these fruits to show my love for you like those diamonds I gave you for your birthday, of all the fruits there is I name this one Melody she loves me a lot I will always be there for her my dearly beloved smiling with her she said your too much jay you did not have to do this for me but thank you for a good time my kids are happy they found a good father ok enough of the fruits when can we talk marriage. I am waiting to hear from the court for the papers and I do not have all the money, yet Melody does not know what she is going to do with me well days, weeks, months went by with her it was like sitting on the beach on some clouds in chairs on top of the sand. Everything was going well a lot of times we would read together dance, sing, and pillow fight also sit in the tub together blowing bubbles at each other in our bubble bath. I was in business with all kinds of people but they were all women my brother Joshua needed somewhere to stay so I let him stay with us, Melody was ok with it so my brother birthday came up so I ask my girlfriend Melody if I could go out with my brother for his birthday and she said ok as long as you come home on time me and him is out to the club we had a good time I drunk a couple of drinks my brother was dancing with all kinds of women [music playing last dragon album "Sysco"-descent] we was out to a strip club named wonderful I couldn't dance with no women I'm telling you I was so in love with Melody I didn't, I couldn't cheat on her I had something so good it was too good to be true well me and my brother come at five am in the morning as soon as l walked in the door Monica punch me dead in my mouth and said where the fuck you been all this time I said baby you said I can go to the club with my brother Jordan for his birthday but she was not trying to hear that because she bust me in my mouth I never seen a woman mad how she saw blood leaking out of my mouth.

This is my second I quarrel with Melody that I had to call the police luckily a police officer came on the scene his name is Sergeant Crawford, she asked me what happen seeing my busted lips I knew her on the block on the corner of 79th street NW 27th avenue she knows I are selling and hustling purses, so I told her what happen to me The police officer said next time a black woman tell you can go out period just do not bring your ass home at five am do not do it because she is worried about you ok, but this is not something to head over heels for why you need a police officer to come out here you are making a big deal out of a small situation and this is your relationship ok I got nothing to do with it. Author, it seems like jay is insecure of keeping a relationship with his new beloved fiancé Melody if you feel the need to call a police on your girlfriend the one that provide for you and make you holy came through for him when he was in the hospital yes, I think the sister is on the right track if her man is out with someone else and not home with her then they will be swinging of her fist across his mouth that is for sure or should I say it slang that is of show' practicing how to speak accordingly but very wise about relationship this is my opinion on this relationship he's having insecurity of their relationship. Back to the police officer don't ever do that again she said you don't want to press charges on your girlfriend because you love her Sergeant Crawford made Melody apologize for hitting Marvin we kiss and make up I was mad because my lip was swollen I had to put ice on it well it was time to go to a party that Mr. Brown had at his house he listens to old school and grown folks me and Melody started to dance right in the middle of the floor holding on to each other we had lots of people jealous because they wanted what we had evil people don't really like to see when two people are in love some of them act funny [envious] I don't agree with everybody at times me and Melody have spirits in us too nobody is perfect we make mistakes, it was negative spirits that made us fight, argue, fuss, and not communicate selfish of each other. We stop letting my brother Jordan stay with us because he did not want to pay his rent for him and his girlfriend they would get into fights out the door they went ok now it was time for Monica's daughter to move in we got along with each other ok but their days we didn't understand her pain, feelings, because I was raise with single parent my father was not there for me I know how Teresa feels however, what I didn't like about her was she would not respect at times if I make a joke or say the wrong things to her she starts flipping, this is how I discipline children I may say sorry but I'm a good father I'm human I say things but don't really mean it, summer came around again a new year in Florida I decided to take them out to the movies, cardinals, and shopping so that they can keep looking beautiful all the time I ran out of money so I told Melody stop by the shop so I can sell some purses and perfumes where we going she said ok right in front of the mall we sell bags, cd's, movies, music I am bringing the clients to me at the mall so I can get something for Thomas.

Melody said we must set positive image on these children, so we used to argue in front of the kids but now we go to church pray read the bible; play video games, watch tv together and do all kinds of things there were times Melody would tell me to stop and I would say no because I want the kids to fun she would take in control this family beautiful liar that's what I said she was there's no mirror on these walls I'm a man that chooses to do right by my girlfriend until we become husband and wife they call me Marvin a man not set up to fall in the way of the wicked when we first got together it was peaches and cream after a few years I started getting weak in love. Melody did not want nobody to tell her how to raise her children Teresa and Thomas I cannot have children it hurts me inside there is nothing more I would like for me to give her my seed, but situations are not the same, Marvin gets better at raising children because he raised his brothers and sisters I have had kids with my ex-wife, and she is ghetto but loving. [brandy Norwood- I do not care] when I was told in all kinds of ways about the children I loved them like they were my own they live under our roof and I had 50 percent say so just as much as the mother did well Melody did not like the fact that I would be out working to late sometimes I stopped she is right I would be out late until 12am and it had to stop. I remember one day I went to work and this women tire went flat she pulled up right by me around the corner of my business she walked up to me ask me to fix her tires me being a nice gentlemen I help her put on the tire after that I sold her my perfumes, purses, trying to persuade her of my upcoming agenda which are movies, cd's and more it was Jane the women I thought was going to be my girlfriend instead it was Melody I told her whenever you support me I do my best to help you back yes, she was driving a Toyota Camry a black vehicle we exchange numbers when she heard my music and saw my purses automatically she bought 10 purses from me I can't believe it she had ask me what's your name? I said Russell do you want to join me in my business you could be my partner I do not have a problem with you. You are a good salesman people at my job listens to these types of music, they were this kind of perfume and watch these movies Jane said I will be back tomorrow alright I will let you know if I have someone thank you. Russell, said before you leave let me give you my card it says it on their R&B, HIP HOP, GOSPEL, RAGGAE and many more I almost fell for her love she was good looking had short hair like Rihanna; skinny like Rihanna; her eyes was captivating I couldn't stop starring I knew if it doesn't work out with Monica I'm going to be with Jane I started singing songs to her like I did Monica then she replied to me do you always sing to your clients I said yes to get them to buy from me lol.

Before you pull out the name of my business is Jay Enterprise now I done said all of that I wonder why wink is coming at me when I am trying to succeed in my business when I was with Melody he called to ask me about Jane, I spoke with Joshua and he says that the nigga is uptight about his girlfriend I said it like t-pain nigga get loose in his music video Jane had told me that she sell fireworks during the 4th of July and she does taxes, real estate, homes, women's lotion, soaps, and fragrance for women she's also trying to put out an ad for women with breast cancer or ovarian cancer as she cut me off jay I have to go but here's my number call whenever you like and we'll conduct business from their Jane had capture the attention from my heart she is the second women I loved since I broke up with my ex-wife Nancy, I told her lets set up a meeting for next week for us to sit down so Jane can look at my profile and demonstration I guaranteed she'll be begging for more. I then said to her have a nice day that's how I hold a women down so she can buy from me or invest into my business compare it to fireworks shooting up into space I think wink is jealous of me my gut tells me he's making a move I'm a let him do that cause I'm with Melody I just won't let him know how fury I am of this criteria customers would send me crazy emails and texts on my phone even the people I've been in business with however, when I came home to Melody and my children every day we kiss before leave home after work I would see Melody and ask her how was your day? She would come home stressed but happy always watching what women would buy from me I grew up on the corner women comes from all over bringing me money I am teaching Melody how to hustle and flow in these streets. I love to make women happy call me crazy but there's no shame in my game I love to sale it's something I'm good at my dreams are to become an actor, writer, a comedian and today is that day I'm hoping this book sales it's about my life how I met Melody and Jane these are my glory in the site of all things I made it to the real world with my work and will never stop me and Melody would get active into social media and be in love by eating with her or letting her feed me fruits tasted sweet I love when she growl and make love to me. They say a way to a man's heart is his soul who can get that respect from her there is no one else refusing to let others come in our heart to rule Melody is someone special to me like when good times roll around when my daughter Teresa call me daddy and my son Thomas would hold hands with me and pray together. Kimberly started getting jealous she would call Marvin three times a day trying to ruin their relationship she was desperate to finding a new man or a good man, Kimberly, needed money for rent knowing that her utility bill was going to expensive her man cheated and left her which is Reggie now it is time for her to make a move. Kimberly went to see her cousin Melody just to see if Marvin would be there since she has been in a struggle luckily he was there when he opens the door surprisingly Kimberly was standing

Chapter 5

alone saying I am sorry can we talk. Kimberly, ask a question are you still working I need miracle in this business give me some wheels [as she talks ghetto] so I can make money you let Melody work for you how about Jane is she hiring now, he said no what happen to your man? Melody is just a teacher she does not have a job neither does Jane then Kimberly kissed him in tears because her life with her kids is ending, so he decided to win her heart like he did Jane told her how beautiful she was one thing led to another they have sex. Afterwards, he told

Kimberly to come around the corner help me sell purses don't say anything to Melody he calls David to tell him ride to the store make sure the register is right, Melody never like Jane cause they're going in business together Melody wouldn't trust Jane let alone Kimberly she didn't think that her own cousin would go that far by sleeping with her fiancé while Melody did not know about the affair she started looking into other things like their next planning trip to Jamaica and family get always. Jane started calling Marvin and Kimberly they were looking for love in all the wrong places wink did not get the attention of the affair with Jane, but he had a hunch that she was sleeping with Marvin he did threat to go to Melody and tell her all things if he did not stop seeing Jane. Jane is a believer she brings good sales at clubs, her job, malls, wherever she went it was her that bought in more money also customers than Jay did, unlikely Melody wanted me to cut Jane off and I said no because that's what pays the bills I couldn't cut other people off that worked for me I told Melody I said baby I'm not going to even lie if you was a salesman in the streets look all kinds of people will call your cell phone leaving nasty text messages, emails, and messages all they want to do is buy from me please understand if the situation was the other way around I would be hurt but I cannot tell you how to run your business, we trust each other enough to know that I'm not cheating ok I still love you baby your co-workers on your job bought purses from me on the street corner and perfumes they also buy cd's and movies alright just believe that I'll never cheat. So, Melody, always argue with me about Jane calling my phone being rude and disrespectful calling me late at night to tell me that they're leaving the corner and she left the key with Joshua Melody woke up asking what did she want I told her she left the key with Joshua my fiancé knew I wasn't sleeping with Jane whenever I used to leave the house I always call her and let Melody know where I'm at if I left the house and came back in ten minutes then I just went to do the groceries or was around the block I was not fucking no one oh to add on to that I'm not a minute fucker, two if I'm fucking or cheating it's going to be for hours and three when I used to walk in the door Melody would say your back baby um that was fast it was only a couple of minutes did you get everything you needed ok Timothy just called here asking for Jane he says that after last night he woke up in the morning and did not see her he said no I do not know where Jane is alright wow you still do not trust me after I proved that I never cheated Melody responded baby I am not blaming you of cheating, but could you call her he says it is important alright. After Melody was done accusing me of cheating I called Joshua to see what he was doing and then lucky came over to bring me some money from the store I told him where the hell is Jane and Kimberly I need the money they made from the store where's my cut he said ask rock cause he collected them last night I went to the game so I told rock I would bring to your house ok Marvin said you good with me [as they stand outside to talk] you hit Kim nigga Jay replied w-h-a-t who told you about Kimberly an- n-a m-a-n I never did that ok Charles gave him a day notice Timothy found out and still holding it down for Jane he's my boy but you became my first partner I'll take care of that with Timothy just say the word [Marvin looking suspicious] leave that bull shit alone I'll take care of wink if got something with me then I'm going to put through his brains how he got his apartment and car he was not alone in this business. Jay, god forgive me for all my sins no one knows I fucked Kimberly not even her ex-boyfriend Reggie know about that night I was committed to Melody like a husband should, and like a father. Whether I am right or wrong I am not a dog now that Kimberly is in business she is supporting me I get 50% of the share how is it a woman can leave and I find her unlike me another man would have neglected, beat, and abuse, hurt, put down talk about all the time with verbal cursing, not being supportive enough, put in too much pain and most of all stepped on. A person can be a treasure to god any man that god gives of her which they prayed for, but to most women a man cannot be a treasure because he is a dog can someone feel my pain.

No, only god can for the bible says god have mercy on whom he has mercy so me and Melody went to every place that you can think of, but she was still curious about the relationship between me and Jane the way she calls me late at night of course my lady was upset but the insecurity starts with me first this is a challenge and I know I will lose this fight. Melody still curious of the affair she says why is she sending you text message and does it have to be violent or nasty he was speechless could not answer she always screen his phone calls and text messages, the only response I gave her was I'm in business with her she's doing what I told her to do which is to pass by her godmother house and wait for me there so I can pick up my cut of the money in the middle of the night we get up arguing about how I'm suppose to do my business right leaving out late in the night is not good people are watching you and they waiting for their next heist you don't want them to take your money why can't she come here. He says wink always think I am on top of you and her at once giving heat about his girl coming over to meet with me then he asks me why you do not walk around the corner and we give it you like that? I said yeah from now on, but the problem is I never wanted us to have malice or envy of a woman because this is how I do business with all my partners so please let me sleep through the night so I can wake up in the morning and go to work. When I go out to make sales in the night I remember Melody telling me it is not good she is just looking out for me so I pulled Melody in the kitchen and said baby I have $34,000 dollars saved in the bank right now for you to keep us from arguing and problem will go away, and you will be happy! Melody looked at me and said no baby keep your business you've been doing this for years this is what you love to do I said you sure because I will give it all up right now I'm dead serious, Melody said baby we not gone argue no more I trust and believe from now on that you will be faithful I told Melody this is not gone stop customers are people period, I told her that this is the reason why I broke up with my ex-wife Nancy because she thought I was having an affair with my co-workers or customers it got to the point where gay men would call me for cologne and purses she thought I was having an affair with them. This relationship is not corrupt ok I want Melody to understand I am the man for her there is no other I came out straight forward and keep the conversation about us I had to deal with our cousin Kimberly she was out of commission I put her at the shop if it is ok with you baby help her alright everyone is going through some shit just knock out the hustle. Hustle me and take me through this bitch but look what happen the tables turn on me again I can't win for losing: we decided to let it go for now until I'm ready to reveal the affair I had with her cousin was a mistake I didn't want her to be hurt my heart cry out when I see women struggle I just want to reach my hands and help them please lord make this easy for me I lived and fought but now I fight no more glory came and got me just wait to you'll see me on billboards and on magazines profit making the world profit me of this the beginning of I can't win for losing when will it all end. I went to Melody mother again she kept accusing me of cheating so I sat down once more with her mother, grandma, I walked into Mrs. Tracy house communicating with her about the courtship we got going through how she thinks I'm unfaithful to her, but I tried to explain this is how I do business I can't just leave my business on the streets I need money, Tracy ask me who is this women and what is her name? I said Jane, then she pats me on the shoulder and said do not worry about your business partners if you know that there is nothing going on between you two then just live your life with my daughter make her happy stop complaining all the time of the insecurities of this wealth cause my daughter just wants what best for the children and the relationship.

So, she turns her back looked at Melody and spoke baby when you are going to get married are you sure that you can handle being in a relationship have give it some thought every time you come home you two just argue about other women do not worry about her you just call the event planner and make some arrangements for a wedding Melody begins to smile momma I am ready for anything I came to ask for support of my wedding but jay says the commission he gets from hustling does not cover ceremonial charges we should just go to court sign the papers and have a small get together Mrs. Tracy sigh [oh, pooh] what you mean a small wedding my baby is not having a small wedding I have to invite people in this party ok get me my black book I have a wedding planner on it [as Melody go upstairs to get the black book] you need to calm down my daughter is looking out for your best interest do not forget that you still on public assistance the way you hustle and the way my daughter work at her school is not the same your benefits criteria does not meet with Melody's you understand you have to come up and leave public assistance Jay kept giving her attitude my public assistance is my business selling purses, movies, perfumes what is wrong with that? You practically bought from me know I am asking you to start supporting us because I only have $35,000 in the bank how much do you want to invest? Tracy screamed at me do not be stupid of this matter my daughter wants a wedding what kind of man are you just wait on god oh the pastor is coming later make sure you do not leave so he can give us our blessing to wed you and my daughter. Melody's grandma gave me soda to drink and food to eat then I laid on the couch waiting for someone to call me for perfumes or cd's Kimberly came over to see if her auntie would buy from her but the purse she had on her shoulder was a Prada, also wearing Gucci shoes, I placed them on the floor next to the table by the door Melody's grandma couldn't believe it she said girl that is a beautiful bag where can I get one I need it for church Kimberly said it's only $40.00 plus the shoes is $100.00 Tracy um uh yeah just put it down I'll buy the shoes from you cause I got to work tomorrow I'm trying to settle this situation with the pastor Melody and Jay are getting married she said oh well I'm proud of you jay where's Melody, Tracy respond she upstairs calling Melody twice where are you bring the black book [as she comes down stairs] Kimberly hey I have not seen you in a while sit down here mama here's your book she said ok [as she gives book to Tracy] Tracy looking for the number to the wedding planner Kimberly having guilt in her heart slipped jay $400.00 from the investment which is his cut he says thank you I was waiting for you all this time then she said rock and lucky will be here later to see you that's what Melody wanted for us to meet in the house ok he says I won't argue Melody's auntie was there Jennifer she's an attorney business is slow at her office as she knocks on the door her eyes glance at the bag on the floor with the shoes Kimberly opens the door with a smile hey how are you? Long time I have not seen my mother pretty she says I like your purse and shoes I know it is $140.00 for both these are the three wise women in our lives Tracy has been married now for 27 years Mrs. Gloria has been married for

Chapter 6

34 years her husband died. Mrs. Evelyn does not have a man, but she has god like the rest of these strong black woman do I sat down in the living room I was so mad and upset I started to cry I told all of them

that Melody still thinks I am cheating on her we stop arguing about it because my tears dried up when I saw the pastor at the front door and Tracy noel was excited she began to praise the lord [as she opens the door] the pastor came in how is everybody doing alright before we start who is getting married in the future? Melody and jay raised their hand the pastor said ok I'm going to pray for the both of you can the two of you please stand in the center of the living room bring me the olive oil [as Kimberly goes for the olive oil] the pastor laid hands over them both Mrs. Gloria put her hands over her mouth saying have Mercy Jesus come down and blessed them o god [as she gets into the spirit] then she started jumping up and down twitching back and forth holy art thou oh Jesus bless their soul oh father and king. (as she shouts) Tracy began to sing oh glory is he; king of all things, oh glory halleluiah king of all things glory halleluiah praise his name Jesus then she stops singing listening to the pastor pray for them. Then the Pastor began prayer father god give us this day that we may speak of his word that will carry you through all things during the rapture of god keep them, protect them, hold them fast in thy bosom make known of their glory oh king for thou art king of all Jews be there guidance, leader don't let them fall into the hands of the adversary but carry them through their lives make them humble that they may profit in this life now and forever more amen. [everybody says it together] reciting Matthews 6:9 our father which art in heaven hollow be thy name thy kingdom come thy will be done on earth as it is in heaven give us this day our daily bread and lead us not into temptation but deliver us from all evil and forgive us for our transgression and trespassing for thine is the kingdom and power, and the glory forever more amen. Mrs. Gloria said now there's no more talk about cheating and infidelities just take your man and kids and do right by each other Mrs. Tracy Noel said I found the wedding planner Keisha Watkins, she does not charge a whole a lot she was the one who did my wedding back in the day and then she pass the business down to her daughter so wait for her to come here (as Tracy pulls the pastor to the kitchen) pastor do you think that my daughter have a future with him he says the lord does not forbade his children for coming to the cross he will not neglect them (while she put out the food) yes, uh a cup of water please [as she pours wine into cup] here thank you for coming to the small party my daughter said she rather go to court sign papers and then go on a honey moon without a wedding I'm the one who convince her to have a decent wedding. However, the pastor convinces of their relationship with the kids he was happy to see that there were not neglected or left alone Pastor Matthew had all the right words spoken of so graciously [speaking in tongues] he said praise god for he is our power everyday he protected the sheep at the door thank you lord. I will make it to the wedding ceremony at the church and then the party I know your daughter is happy {while they're talking} Jane walks in with wink he gave jay a hug telling him congrats on your newlywed ok, Jane hugs Melody telling her I know you have insecurity about me and jay but it's just work were not having a relationship or an affair believe in yourself trust your man don't be afraid of us I'm only human [as Kimberly feeling the guilt she went upstairs to check on kids] as she went into the room asking her son is everything ok do you want some food; he says yeah I want food Kimberly says come downstairs they preparing the table. Then she went to use the bathroom holding her tears back not shouting of Melody's relationship she says when one door closes the other one opens I know they will be a man out there for me I am not jealous my feelings for Jay is mutual [as she talks in the mirror] keeping quiet of their affair. Mrs. Betty, Told jay baby you keep doing the right thing if someone say you doing wrong let them talk their garbage you just pray Evelyn looked at me and said jay you taking care of those children and Monica that is a good sign [tone: happy] I cried in tears cause this is what I call support even if it's words I can adapt my life with Melody her family are very sweet oh my cousin Francis came by just to say congrats on the newlyweds and he brought flowers then me and him talked in the back yard [while Kimberly is setting the table] Monica wanted everyone around the table for the blessing, during that time Francis told jay are sure we can trust wink so he won't talk jay says I don't think he's that desperate to ruin our relationship and besides I paid for his house, car, clothes, all of that will say bye, bye, the minute he opens his mouth about me and Kimberly as grandma was upstairs looking out the window ease dropping on conversation could not believe it was her granddaughter marrying this man in a couple of weeks she kept her mouth shut. Therefore, they were talking to me Melody walked in and her mother walked up to her and said you know this man sleeping around on you, you need to stop hating because he is a good man. Afterwards, we left and went home a couple days later the arguing stopped and calm down then Melody feeling insecure started right back up again Marvin feeling resentful went to the pastor at the church to ask for counseling on relationships between him and Melody it was not us Melody said it is the women that she does not trust anyway she is supposed to be with her man just receive the money from the business and then tell goodbye cause you have me. Marvin tries to end the probable cause by calling his friend Jane on her cell phone in front of Melody to say bring the money please my girl is tripping she thinks we are getting together but I told her no I would not destroy our relationship or our wedding she said your girlfriend has a problem and I am going to fix it for her she needs to keep my name out her mouth I do not give a damn about her insecurity I hate that shit I will be over there. However, when Jane came over to bring me my cut of the profit she told me that in a couple of weeks she might be moving her job is moving but she will keep in touch every month Jane will fly down to give me my cut of the profit for my business I agreed but what will wink think is he ok with it, Jane did not respond. Me and Charles, Joshua, Timothy and Samuel, decided to play ball at the courtyard and they said how can you have a relationship if Melody is insecure about you, as a matter fact you did cheat on her with Kimberly whose next Jane lol. {while the boys play ball and laughing at Jay} he says how about I call Jane to prove we never slept with other, Charles, Timothy, look startled gazing to see if Jane would listen wink always had the hots for Jane when he first laid eyes on her. As he calls her house phone Jane, answered "hello" whose this Marvin I'm calling because I'm out here playing ball with my boys I want you to let them know that were not sleeping with each other the boys lol do you think Jane can eat Melody out since Melody is insecure about her man (laughing) Timothy says I know you put Kimberly in your mind first thinking of her [Marvin quickly hangs up with Jane] he didn't want her to hear that while they are in the basketball field Kimberly calls Marvin telling him to meet me at John's Pizza for the drop off. But Marvin is still with his boys so wink catch an eye Jay envious of him so Charles Joshua wanted Jay to know that Melody is old school, and he should move on to Jane. However, wink always love Jane since she started working around the corner. Timothy didn't want Marvin to know the hatred had for Marvin, he tried to get evidence on his best friend he knew that if Melody finds out that Kimberly had sex with Marvin their relationship is over wink spoke to him and his boys using the slogan "time waits on no man soon glory will catch his faith, fire will consume the corruptible" as he holds the ball in his hands at the ball court afterwards, he walks off the court. Ball bounces itself lucky running after wink to discuss a word with him {Mariah Carey- there for me} rock holding jay back "just leave it maybe he wants to be alone" go home Marcus get your women some flowers or take her out on a date. I couldn't sleep I was talking to all kinds of people over the phone I was going out to clubs sitting down by myself drinking sometimes being dead drunk I came home to tell Melody that I'm a dog there days I fall through the sink people don't like me because I establish even when I did good to them hey telling her let's get married please baby that's how I know our love is strong, so I decided to leave Melody didn't realize what I was doing while I was drunk I went to visit Jane at her house and she had wink over there when she had open the door I saw him sitting on the couch, then I ask the question when are you two love birds planning a wedding Jane replied were not ready for that are you drunk oh my god Timothy get some water telling Jay to sit on the couch as he limps to the

Chapter 7

couch saying, I am sorry Jane for busting over your crib, but we must talk what the hell wink doing here I saw him at the basketball court m-a-n what is going on?

Wink decided to call Jay's cousin Francis to tell him come get your cousin Jay he's drunk sitting on my lady's couch we had something going before he walked in Jay cried himself to sleep until Francis came in to pick him up Jay dreaming of when he had seizures and Jane would be there to take care of him but now things have change Jay sometimes would pee on himself from having seizures no one understands why Jay choose to be the way he is insecure of himself keeping thoughts of him and Melody has really got him to destruction maybe Marvin will pick up on his strength wink said I'm going outside to wait for Joshua, and Francis they coming over to pick him up I think something happen with him and Melody after he left that's when Jay woke up saying did you ever have dreams Jane said what is going on with you and Melody Jay tighten up ok it's not that bad your getting married in a couple of weeks why are you getting drunk and talking about dreams Jay replied all I wanted was a good woman have children and be a good husband and a father live happy forever, money or stars can't by that these things are not for sale when they are in god hands, mind, body, soul and highly love what's your dream? Jane just listens to what he had to say but she is feeling strongly for wink Jay we cannot be together, but I know your always alone so when you go home be good with your wife do not hate she just wants what best for you. Jay said my uncle told me Jay you not going to never keep a woman with the type of business you running first of all let me remind you that your handsome and good looking you could get any women if you want to, second you got plenty of money don't be afraid to marry a pretty good women, thirdly you have too many good things going on in your life at one time just take it slow one day at a time, don't worry about what people say marry your women and be happy with her. Author, I do think that jay is having cold feet because he doesn't know what wink will say at the wedding a long time friend turned corrupt over a women in the book of Jared X it says when thou has found a good women always remember to speak good words of the truth let her and the children know who god is what it means to have power control the inhabitants of your life, keeping your feet from sin I believe getting counsel from the father relieves the stress of making mistakes therefore, this book speaks of poverty and relationship of how to deal with each other for Judah mourn and the gates there of languish America is always in mourning but you have become a true believer instead of an adversary make known of it to the world let everyone say this is god. Marvin said one thing I did not like is when Melody let her cousin Kimberly move in our house and she set me up to get robbed by her boyfriend I will never make that mistake again not even with David her cousin. My own race and color are the ones to do me wrong, but god forgive them sorry for saying this but there is good and bad in everything that we do, I choose to be equal with him god the father listens to me they pulled their guns on me right back at them what goes around comes around that is the life cycle one day they gone need me and neither me nor Melody will be there. Jay told his father I had $3,000 dollars in my pocket they pulled out an aka gun on me and a 9 clock ran out the car jumped on top of Melody's car as she drove off with Kimberly on top of the car telling her to get off I called the police because Tony and Reggie got in the car going after Melody but they jumped and beat me up with their fists, hands, and guns and while they was doing it they said they couldn't stand me because I was getting money and they wasn't; Kimberly felt shine because she doesn't Melody to know she slept with Jay he felt afraid of losing Melody so he gave them whatever she ask for. Well anyway Melody went to jail because her cousin Kimberly was on probation and she called the police on Melody she went to jail but I bond her out Melody had a paid lawyer unfortunately, Melody won the case because Kimberly lied about what happen at the scene I give Melody credit for being strong and applaud Kimberly for not telling Melody about the affair in court I probably deserve punishment but I was not ready to tell Melody anyway she will always be my wife I'll never forget who my children are and my wife even though I cheated it was one time I gave her my all Melody she's like a rainbow as we get in the car I told Melody what happen to me when I went to sale out there in the corner I said a man walked up to me he looked at me and said can you show me your purses and cologne for men I said sure Jay was very relentless he was not expected to get robbed again the man pulled out a 357 magnum he said give me all your money now I had made one thousand dollars in my pocket I took the money out and gave it to him he still shot me he said to me fuck nigga don't come back on this corner no more pussy ass nigga I could not believe that he was standing right there and robbed me he shot me I was bleeding and yelling, screaming I was almost paralyzed because the bullet was near my spine and it is still in my back until this day. Melody was there in my heart I thought she was gone get shot I was afraid, but I did not want her to die for me. I was holding onto her while I was bleeding thinking of Melody my life with her is over she will find another man like me I do not know if the kids are going to remember me and if they will appreciate what I have done for them so far taking Melody to the restaurant to eat before we pick up the kids from school I want to show her that I love her. I remember that is the same guy that pointed the gun at Melody and said get back bitch he left drop the money on the floor running for his life I can see it now blood was everywhere Melody crying screaming just leave us alone I am happy they did not kill her thank you Jesus she is my proud and joy I remember seeing lights blue and red Metro Dade Police came to the scene to ask what happen they next time we will not come out here to do a police report ok you need to open a shop to sell your purses alright I went to the hospital and Melody drove the kids home don't worry baby people get jealous I will pray for them I pass out in the hospital when I woke up Melody was still there for me she was happy to see me wake up I touch her hand telling her let's get married for the fall and move out of state I always say it but never act upon it so what do you prefer we do she said well the officer said we didn't lose all of our money they found $700.00 on the scene she said thank god your ok yeah it's enough for us to move the investigator wanted to ask questions because it could be gang related and Melody spoke up and said my cousin Kimberly was involved and I did press charges against there is a case pending in court I transferred all my cases downtown and she showed it to the detective he ok let me get this down before I do that let me get your ID plus who are you to Marvin she said I'm his fiancé oh he said congratulations is your cousin Kimberly living with you Melody said no she moved out ever since her cousin David, and Reggie robbed us and pulled out a gun on me and my children plus Jay. The police officer did say he was on the street corner selling bags, perfumes, and bags well we asking the question is it legal and she said yes legal aid attorney located on Biscayne Blvd. jay decided to respond to the police officer excuse me I never do things illegal my attorney hook me up I paid him for public assistance I do have my card and ID after he gave him all the information yes officer I am working on that getting a store front but I don't have any money I'm still on welfare I sale purses every week making less than a $100.00 but in my heart, mind, I know who set me up it be the ones that smile in your face that knows you very well the man who worked on the side of me was Joshua and he told me that wink set you up after I left the hospital I went back on the corner with my boys to tell them I might be moving my business elsewhere while in pain, hurting, Melody was there she heard Joshua saying it was wink I couldn't believe my ears when I heard this [he sigh] it's a problem ok um, Joshua describe briefly what Timothy was saying about how Melody's grandmother heard the conversation during the small gathering I said m-a-n [smiling] let me cut you off and say nothing happen we just talked and that was it. [music playing Tinashe- in case we die, 2012] 20 people working around the block the day I got hurt wink walked up to me smiling saying you want something to eat nigga let me say you don't mess with god's children you know what I mean never put his children in danger for it will come back to you, as I was standing I got a call from Juan he said we on 70th street and 15th avenue. Timothy almost got shot he was trying to sell purses and cd's, movies, and some cars drove by and started shooting instead his baby mother got shot she was with him at the corner of millers it was a different corner store they aim it at wink but he duck down his baby mother was pregnant with two twins she was having girls, she died there on the scene Timothy got in his car to get the plates and make, model of the car they called the police about what they saw but Timothy lost his family and his girl Jane she didn't know he had another women besides Timothy was going to tell her that Jane was for him and he's living with her when he came to me after processing and pressing charges against who killed his girlfriend that's when I met him I said I forgive you he couldn't even look me straight in the eye he was just crying what goes around, comes around, now were even I saw another friend of his he goes by the name of Donald which set me up I told him when I saw I loved him if I was the man I use to be I would of paid to have these people kill him or do it myself but I change from that man long time ago I'm not the same anymore; my evil ways has turn over into love a lot of people has told me I was crazy I said no I'm just following my heart, mind, soul I became a believer in him Christ Jesus which gave me my mother, and a women a beautiful women to call my own she always reminded me that when Jesus gives you a chance after chance your chance may run out cause you played with yourself and your not ready, when you're not ready you don't know what's coming your way because what is ready to come you don't know cause god is in your life your able to survive Christ said don't judge the meek those that worship me do it in spirit and in truth [Q music Chris brown-don't judge me] wink had responded no one keep secrets if we provoke someone then let them be ashamed of their sins in this life you reap what you sow because after I was robbed by Tony, David and Quasha, Melody's family a few days later somebody came back to the house and shot the house up and they was almost killed! Now this is what happens when you mess with god's children. I let Jane know all these things that was happening to me because I needed someone to talk to and it was too much pressure my cousin Francis was telling Melody you've been set up me and jay don't think Melody had something to do with it she goes to work and then picks up the kids from school m-a-a-n listen wink what's the problem why you tripping just do your business nigga Melody is not money hungry cause she work as a teacher so why did it end up like this Joshua, Charles, Timothy, Juan been with plenty of bitches and ho's I can't believe Timothy falling for Jane she mean a lot to you go ahead be with her then but leave jay out of it, it's like this a women respect herself the way she gives god respect clean; very calm and decent will not betray a man for his money the thought of many women are their minds the beauty of many women are their looks. Coming out of prison from time to time I think the only person to respect is god not just money, as Francis confronts wink about the affair outside in

Chapter 8

the car letting him know that it was just one time do not be carried away they are not having an affair Melody means a lot to Marvin so give him his space. Living with Jane was good at first but turned out to be hell the grass is not always green Francis ask a question were was Kimberly Timothy look at Jane mad cause he doesn't want Jane to leave him he'll do anything to be with her then he told Marvin play on, playa, this is your game you do one holding the ball so what you going to do hate on wink, Marvin look surprise curious of the fact that Jane would go to Timothy and Melody will leave him he decided to come clean with Melody baby sit down there is something we need to discuss relationships I have (looking regretful) with another women was not with Jane, Melody, drop her hands on the side w-h-a-t she said tell me who then? He said it was with Kimberly as tears came down his eyes Melody feeling like she lost her man, she fires back by saying "I'm pregnant" doctor is said it is impossible through the grace of god I am. He said it was one time she slapped him yelling why haven't said anything ever since we almost got killed cause of your affair she grabbed him and kissed him "don't let it happen again let's love each other, forget Kimberly she use people a lot" I'm glad we kicked her out I won't tell Reggie my mouth is close so he won't get mad at us I'm trying to realize what has got into Reggie he never did these things before as Marvin feeling regretful he says Timothy found out now he wants to stab me in the back because he loves Jane I never came between them, but I helped her so she can take care of her family. Melody let us get married and move to a better place how about New York city it is a good idea we will get to go on broadway theatre with the kids and grow our family. Baby as much as I love the streets I agree as they kiss and make love. Author speaking from the heart, I think it was about time that Jay tells Melody about their true love affair Melody being faithful and Marvin loves women every time he goes to the street corner to sell purses, perfumes, movies he slips off with some women he just can't help himself as much as he tries to grow his business it was just falling through the cracks now the next morning going back to the character dirty red working the corner with Timothy saw Jane seeing how Timothy pulls on Jane he says "hey let me talk to you," Jane says what beef you have with my friend business while it's slow for me there's no customers Marvin decided to help me Samuel said fuck that you was sleeping around cheating on wink with your ex-boyfriend give me your number baby look at me as he pulls condoms out his pockets telling her sweety I'm not a bad person theirs is a hotel come here [as he drags her in the car drives to the hotel while Timothy is at the block ahead selling movies] I want you to feel my power and how it splashes out with goodness. Timothy kissing Jane I have money baby do not leave me alone in here give some love as she tries to fight him off be common let down your hair as they undress she look at him and said I will make sure Timothy bust your head open [tears] her brown skin coffee complexion with cream and sugar makeup on glowing even in the shadow they make love, having sex. As Marvin brings his thoughts together about himself he says in his mind I have been through it all and come to peace of my mind from all what I have been through. When I lived with Jane her daughters didn't like me because they thought I was taking money out their pockets but I came in business with their mother with my own money I paid for her to come around the corner and sell purses, perfumes, colognes, movies her kids were mature enough to understand so they were jealous that me and their mother would get along by making money on the street corner Jane saw me arguing with her kids she decided to stop me and say wow hold your horses R. Kelly who the hell you think you are arguing with my kids on the street corner they have a father if you claim that you're a good man and a father to Melody's kids then why are you screaming at my kids? Are you crazy did you forget everything the pastor thought you during your courtship with Melody he says your kids said that I was taking money from you they don't understand but me and you have been in business over a year now you know the routine she responded in a ghetto way yeah mother—k I told my kids tax business is due I pay every month cause your helping me grow my business at the job ok don't give you a reason to yell at my kids he was very angry gave her one look come here let me talk to you as they go on the side to talk you and wink has put my relationship in a bind Melody could not trust me working my business let alone your kids just keep 100 alright from now on bring me my money I should not have to chase you down for my bread you dig go find your man before I put it to you right and make you regret it. Jane, [tears] alright I see how it be I thought you loved me Marvin what happen to you're the love of my life before Melody boo there was Jane you be coming over my house drunk and shit talking about your problems to me Jay tries hard to hold back his guilt he says get the f--- out my face before I make you taste these bananas I don't give a fu—about Timothy he could kiss my ass actually, her two daughters Cynthia and Malorie was standing their looking at us I was stabbed by her kids in the back in this business when I was not looking I was hit in the head the same mistake will not happen twice I was bleeding in love for Jane but not Melody is my priority back in the day I had to get 18 stitches in my head I was admitted and had 6 seizures I was out for two weeks straight. Malorie busted out all my windows in car because she found out I slept with Kimberly Marian tried to stop her but Malorie called her boyfriend John close the police station after I left the hospital he decided to slap me because I hurt Melody, it was Melody that called the police for aggravated assault Jane scream stop hating this business will still be good with or without you. Terry was shock he said from the corner and into an actual store, the police took him to jail for assault Joshua rushed to the scene just to see if his friend is ok Jane apologize to Marvin and said I am sorry I really do not want us to fight over me kids or about money, bills, and I am controlling myself me and Timothy has decided to make things work go ahead get good with what you have your family, peace I am out. Jane is not accusing me of sleeping with Melody she knows our relationship is strong she choose to accept that this is why I pray for those people who have a kind heart Melody became more loving and less worried she knew that Marvin was into gang related issues but Jay is growing out of it all because of a women that he didn't even spend time with him and Jane only talk after she left work she would come around the corner just to sell purses, movies, perfumes Jane did bring in a lot of customers and she was sincere hey this is why Marvin could not let her go she had skills. Jane had left her gun in my car she forgot it I never saw underneath the seat of the car son one day cops pulled us over the shoulder and ask for driver license, registration, and title of the car they were checking for drugs Melody pulled over I heard over the pa to check for drugs instead he found a gun in the car I said maybe it belongs to Jane I told the police officer that Jane must of drop it or left it in our car we gave her a ride home the other day, the gun was registered to her Jane had thought someone stole it or the kids must of took it to school to their friends after the police officer had verified my story he detained us for possession of gun in the car. I couldn't tell her where I was going she thought I went back to Melody to explain about our moving leaving

Jane was hard, Melody was having second suggestion of moving she says is this a joke we helped Jane and she set us up my plan was to go see my godmother Diana but cops arrested me the police officer told me that Jane reported it stolen and they couldn't find it now when we get to the station [police officer telling us what to do] you'll be charged with a concealed weapon he [Jay] cried when will the violence stop will it ever be straight as he sigh, calling for help oh one more thing officer can you please let my friend know I'm going to prison to pick up the car and bond me out please (as they get into police car) the police officer drives to the station; he says sure I could do that for you. Melody made a decision to call Daniel for money to bail her out and jay, Daniel couldn't believe his eyes when he saw Melody he says "damn I can't believe they got arrested" after they've been relieved from the police station Melody and Jay took a ride back home where they found their car Thomas and Teresa came out the house just to give them a hug saying mother I heard you were arrested is everything ok momma she replied yes baby we alright Melody and Jay kiss he says thank you for bailing me out Melody couldn't help herself she said tell me it's over between you and Jane I'm getting tired of the old sad stories he says yes it's finally over I had a

Chapter 9

short talk with her as a matter fact my business with Jane is cutting. As they were going inside their home Melody suggested leave all your bad friends they do not love you or care for you it is just us now work on being a family we are now poor this is the third time I bail you out Daniel had to help both of us with this bill.

The next week I went to court the judge drop the charges with the fire arm being stolen because Jane did not come to testify only charge they gave me was the gun was in my possession as a x convict I broke up with Jane and stayed with Melody we visited her godmother Diana for a while we talked and eat she fed us grill chicken with cheese, peach cobbler, stream beans, squash soup, and macaroni with cheese, rice, oxtail, vegetables, garlic bread hell me and kids were hungry I never had good food we always go out to eat then it hit me how much she loved us coming into the truth about relationships you have to learn how branch a family tree create some type of way to endure in this life come to terms of yourself before you can judge somebody else, how can I be so stupid putting Melody through my trials, no more pain and suffering now we are changed I know I've said it but now I'm acting it my godmother loves us to cook this many food praise the lord and savior I took some food home. When we got home I pray for everyone in my household thank you Jesus for waking me up every morning keeping me in check before we left her house she ask us when is the wedding we told her in two weeks me and Melody has worked out a plan to have a business opened up in our name we provided our souls to our church they have helped us by giving these words which are calming of the spirit yes we're planning on getting married at the hold for hunting house, weber church at Matthews garden up in LA, California the guest list is 100 people we like it because it has a vineyards, a chateau where we can do the ceremony and then everybody goes inside for the party they will set up tables, chairs, music, food, and etc. I lived with Melody for a while now and I think it is time we start believing in ourselves before we can make that big step which is to become husband and wife for life. Diana replied I would like to see the church if the wedding planner can make a way for me to arrive on time and be seated Melody said there will be chairs for you and the whole family it is just jay I want him to work on his capability on how to greet customers, people, family, what to say to the pastor, and learn his vows so that I will not look bad. After we had left me and Melody went home with the kids I was shock by what she said I grabbed her kiss her made Melody feel good then I said get ready for me while I put the kids to sleep, when they fell asleep me, and Melody decided to go in our rooms under sheets I undress she helped me then we made love. (Keri Higson-make love) the next morning I woke up took a shower then went to the church to get counseling from our pastor I had to pay the price for leaving Melody alone, but he said do not worry about a thing take it slow and you will see how quick changes can be made I respected Melody a lot and her god because she proves me wrong every time I had a problem I went to her, so she deserves this wedding no matter what happens to me I want her to be happy. Later on I went back for the kids to take them to counsel from god the father I really want them to grow spiritual understand the way of this world completing all things through his words, [tears] blood came from eyes but now it turned into water there's no more blood from eyes I can see clearly now that my problems has went away I'm not perfect if I see a gorgeous woman then my heart will fall but if I sustain a decent women then my heart will never fail me I am confident of this. Author, I believe Marvin is ready to grow out of his ghetto hood boy and come into ghetto fabulous which means producing more value in a relationship making the world know how to deal with your situations and be ready for more challenges redeeming life of its own, achieving more goals, completing more values, taking chances not failing to prove thyself; worried of others but cannot support himself changing the talk, mind of many people that did not believe Jay has knocked out the hustle by patting his self on the back giving less worries and more rejoicing in his heart, making the children know that it's ok to make mistakes you just have to correct them. Me and Melody decided to always get family therapy at our church, just when we said that we would work out our problems Melody love to argue about women because I forgot to get down on one know and propose to her in front of the pastor, Melody got loose during the therapy sessions because Marcus had never propose I thought he found another women he said no where's my manners I've been out of commission but I'm working on getting a ring believe me [with regret] he looks sad, bitter couldn't talk cause his motivation was about moving to New York City, and opening a store front with great ambition his good was to always make Melody happy. He said we still need counseling from our pastor while we work on our courtship there are some things we must tighten up before the wedding day I want nothing in my chest if you have anything to say come out with it now [as Marvin lied about the ring he had it in his pocket; he just wasn't ready to propose yet] the next week it was made official they got married, moved to NYC in the big apple she was very confident of their relationship and yes it's a girl our baby was born on the big apple, her name is Jeanette Marsha Gonzalez god gave her to me I'll watch her grow nice mocha skin complexion I'm not sleeping at Jordan's house or my car now me and Melody can afford a house in the big apple my auntie Evelyn lives up two blocks from our house so I drop the kids off to school and my auntie off at work me and Melody open a store front our baby Jeanette came with

Chapter 10

us the same thing I sold in Miami, FL I had in my store purses, perfumes, movies, cd's, cologne for men, socks, shoes, etc. We decided to work an honest job on our feet all day until 9am-4pm finally, I can come home without no arguing Melody comes home to me every night I am her only man we lived with our new baby I save money for college for all my kids. I did not see Jane anymore she used to see me sleeping at burger king looking dirty, tired, then she used to tell me "I want to see you get a good life never let a good woman go," I remember telling the kids me and Melody are not arguing anymore, and we worked out our differences. The relationship I had with Kimberly has swallowed itself because now she doesn't have a man or a place to stay her cousin kicked her out and her mother can have Kimberly in the house without no job when I was trying to help her overcome her fears of achieving new goals, and standards that bitch didn't want hear it so now I get the last laugh she called Melody bursting in tears about how her beat her and threw her things out the house Melody was very hurt by the way she would steal from me and have her boys jump us pointing a gun Melody decided to hang up the phone, she looked at me and said baby give me a kiss while my daughter was there in her crib I kissed her and made her lemonade it's a metaphor meaning she taste good like lemonade there is no one else but Monica we take chances with each other by going out on Broadway looking at movies, shopping, going on rides, me and her went to Dave and Busters just to chill with the boys although, I left Miami Joshua, Charles, Juan, Francis, and yes Jane came to see me at the restaurant I ask where's Timothy they said that nigga left the box long time ago he's no longer with us. I was surprised in mourning because he was jealous but I hang in there for money that he would make selling my products, rejoice came when I saw Jane we put our troubles behind us she told her life is getting better she found someone else and they working on a wedding she's been with him for almost 2 years now she told I feel like I'm ready to become a mother all over again I said I learn from family therapy sessions Melody was right it helps me with my anger and my frustration not making money is one thing but losing a relationship, being alone, in the ghetto is not cute so I change my personality and gave up the hood ghetto boy now I'm a man. In this life there was opportunity for me chasing after my dreams to carry a wonderful woman and become something besides a salesman I did say that my brother Samuel came to see me with Terry they got a role for me to play in the title of it is "think like a man" it's a movie that will come out soon I've been wanted to put out my book it was hard for me to find someone like Edith Novinsky to revise it and publish my book. I am sorry for the pain I cost my mother and father but now that we as a family are rich I will propose a toast and drink to my future as an actor one day you will see at the Oscars, or the Emmy's promoting my book I am not afraid to face many challenges of uplifting others showing them how I have made it let other people invest into their own future just like Melody showed invest into your own future rather it be writing, speaking, whatever satisfied your heart never say never just same way I got over Jane and Kimberly I know anybody can get over their fears of trying and do it. Make life easy for you go to church pray that all things come to you on a silver platter I say gold because with it you can do all things through Christ no one needs to know your business or agenda but they can buy my book which is easy you can order it or google online the very same day I saw Melody Jane was standing there I didn't know what to do yes, I was torn between two I loved but you can't always have two choose between one or the other, I did the right thing I gave myself a chance of becoming a father being there for Teresa, Thomas, Jeanette, means a lot to me now that she's walking after 18 months I'm lucky to have Melody (while he's jumping up and down in his living room) I live at an apartment for $1million dollars 7 bedrooms 4 bathroom I have my own bathroom my own car thanks to people like

Sierra Diamond which found the author to promote my book which is me Jay Gonzalez I never thought that this would be hard. Marian came to see me and he says let me help you with your new role I'll be your driver since you made it I miss you bro he hugged me crying saying I'm proud of you I knew you could do better I never gave up on you, m-a-n everybody is talking about this book I bought it online amazon. com family, children, co-workers, I can't believe it you finally achieve everything you said Melody is a lucky women to have someone like you how is your daughter Jeanette [tears of joy] he came up at my front doors walked in to my house saw my family and said I'm proud of you my father walked in to surprise me (I cried loud) saying oh my god Christ bless me once more to see my father here I told him jay came out the hood he looked me in the eye and said you're not ghetto no more now you're a man jay you have found you a good women don't ever leave her remember you have a family now it's no more just you share your life with others I bought gifts the next person honk his horn roll down his window hey is Marvin their I said nigga come inside he pulled up my drive way Juan and Benjamin brother I can't believe you come all the way to see me he said congratulations on your new book I came to help you and take you out to the club we go hang with the boys maybe go to Dave and Busters I said actually you guys can come with me to the casino that is where I will do book signing for my fans I'm on Facebook people are logging onto my book right now and because you have supported me in this business drinks are on me tonight. Bring it in close (as they pour themselves Champagne in a glass) they make a toast, pooh yeah. (Keri Hilson ft. Akon "change me")

The End.

Printed in the United States
by Baker & Taylor Publisher Services